P9-ASK-410

Presented to

_____

from

_____

_____

_____ 19 _____

Dear Parents:

Looking for favorite or unusual trucks is a fun game that young children often enjoy playing while riding in the car. This simple story introduces and identifies many of the trucks your child is likely to see. As you read the story, you may want to point out some of the interesting features of each truck. You can help your child discover the similarities and differences among these trucks.

We consider books to be gifts that encourage a lifelong love of reading. We hope you enjoy reading along with Barney and BJ as they discover trucks.

Mary Ann Dudko, Ph.D.
Margie Larsen, M.Ed.
Early Childhood Educational Specialists

Art Director: Tricia Legault
Designer/Illustrator: Joseph Hernandez

Printed at ColorDynamics, Allen, Texas 75002

Distributed in the U.S. by Lyrick Publishing.

2 3 4 5 6 7 8 9 10   00 99 98
ISBN 1-57064-128-5
Library of Congress Number 97-70880

Barney's
Book of
Trucks

Written by Monica Mody
Illustrated by Joseph Hernandez

BJ loves to play with trucks. "Vroom! Vroom!"
"Let's go and take a look at some real trucks,"
says Barney.

Joe's Corner

Fresh
Foods
Delivery

**Delivery
truck**

Telephone
Company

**Telephone
truck**

U.S. Mail

**Mail
truck**

In the neighborhood, Barney and BJ see
many trucks.
"Yum! Yum!" says BJ. "The ice cream truck
is my favorite"

Gardener's
truck

Ice Cream
truck

Produce
truck

Lives
tru

Grain
truck

Hay
truck

Johnny's
Apples

Milk truck

Pickup truck

Trucks do a lot of work on farms.
"The tank on the milk truck is filled with milk,"
says Barney.
"Wow, that is so much milk!" exclaims BJ.

Foam pumper truck

Baggage truck

Scissors truck

At the airport, trucks are busy all day and night.
A scissors truck lifts food up to the plane.

Fuel truck

Rocks come tumbling out of the dump truck.
The cement mixer churns the cement.

Cable carrier

Grapple truck

Crane truck

Tractor-trailer
truck

The big rigs haul heavy loads. They are made of two parts: the tractor and the trailer. Sometimes they are called semis.
"Aye yie yie! I counted 18 wheels!" shouts BJ.
"That's an 18 wheeler," says Barney.

Moving truck

Logging truck

Double trailer truck

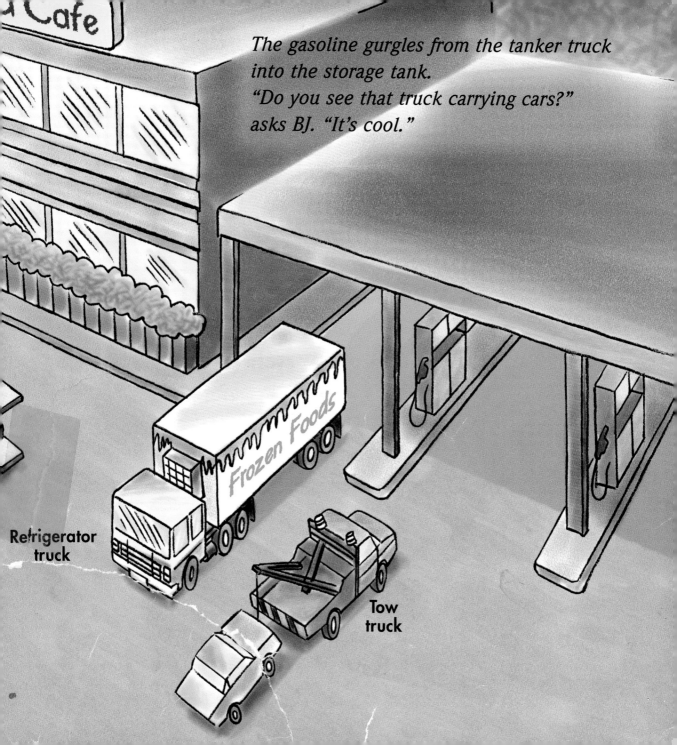

The gasoline gurgles from the tanker truck into the storage tank.
"Do you see that truck carrying cars?" asks BJ. "It's cool."

Refrigerator truck

Tow truck

Cafe

Frozen Foods

Street
sweeper

Ambulance

Fire
truck

Recycling
truck

Garbage
truck

Armored
truck

Hardwo

"These sure are noisy trucks!" shouts BJ.
"They are important helpers for us,"
says Barney.

Antique
fire engine

The tractor pulls a decorated flatbed trailer.
"Hooray! A parade!" shouts BJ.

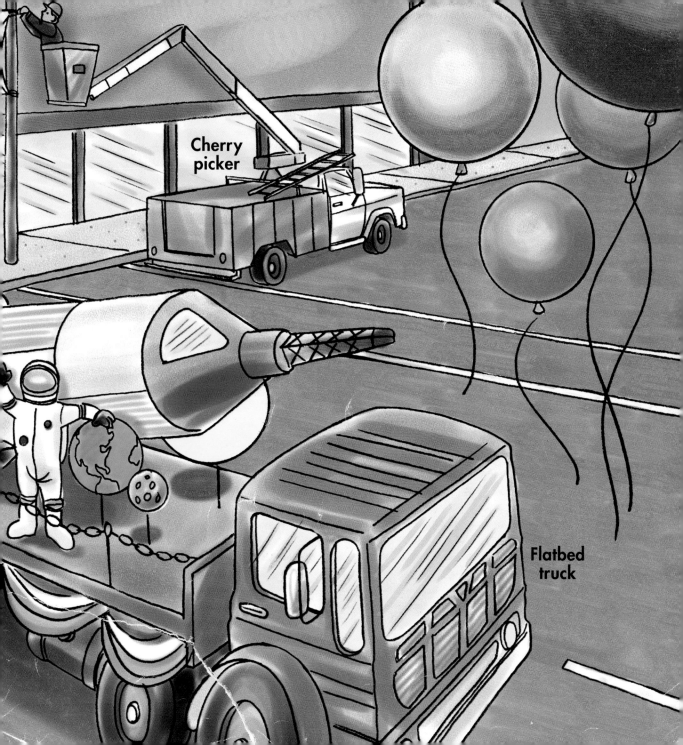

Cherry picker

Flatbed truck

"Do you have a favorite truck?" asks Barney.
"Trucks can do so many different things,"
says BJ. "I love them all! Vroom! Vroom!"

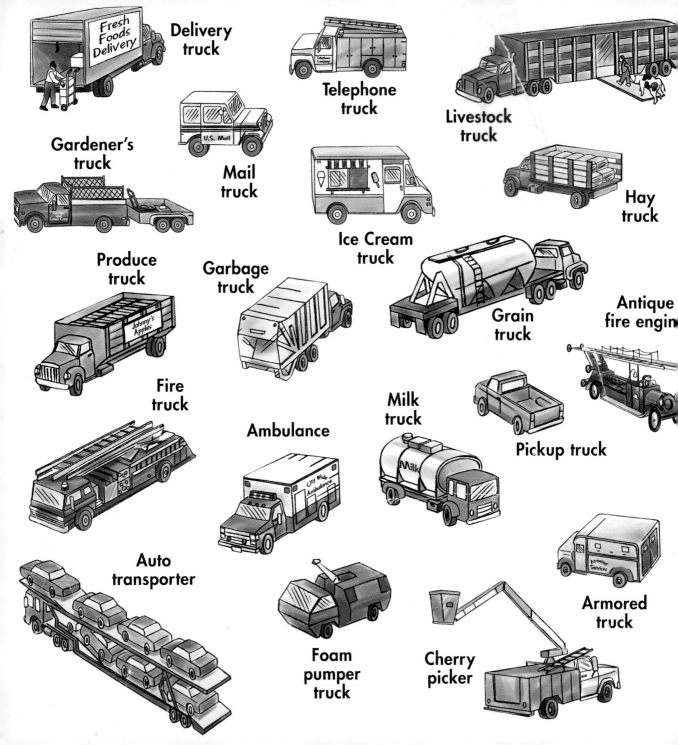

Delivery
truck

Telephone
truck

Livestock
truck

Gardener's
truck

Mail
truck

Hay
truck

Ice Cream
truck

Produce
truck

Garbage
truck

Grain
truck

Antique
fire engine

Fire
truck

Milk
truck

Ambulance

Pickup truck

Auto
transporter

Armored
truck

Foam
pumper
truck

Cherry
picker

LIZARDS

THE REPTILE DISCOVERY LIBRARY

Louise Martin

Rourke Enterprises, Inc.
Vero Beach, Florida 32964

Library of Congress Cataloging-in-Publication Data

Martin, Louise, 1955-
  Lizards.

  (The Reptile discovery library)
  Includes index.
  Summary: An introduction to the lizard
family — how they look, where they live,
and what they eat
  1. Lizards—Juvenile literature. [1. Lizards.]
I. Title.
II. Series: Martin, Louise, 1955-
Reptile discovery library.
QL666.L2M33   1989   597.95   88-30678
ISBN 0-86592-577-1

TABLE OF CONTENTS

LIZARDS

There are twenty different families of lizards, and these families contain over 2,800 **species**. These include the large monitor lizards, tiny geckos, iguanas, chameleons, and skinks. True lizards belong to the family Lacertidae. They are found only in Europe, Africa, and Asia. Most of the North American lizards belong to the iguana and skink families.

This black girdle-tailed lizard lives in South Africa

HOW THEY LOOK

Like most **reptiles**, lizards have a rough, scaly skin. From time to time they grow too big for their skins and shed them. This is called **molting**. There are many varieties of lizards. Some are brightly colored, and others are colored to match their surroundings. Lizards that live in desert areas often grow spiky horns on their heads and tails.

These spiky lizards are called stargazers

WHERE THEY LIVE

Lizards are most common in hot or warm countries. Because they are cold-blooded, lizards need to lie in the sun to warm themselves. This means they cannot live in very cold places like the Arctic and Antarctic. Although many kinds of lizards can swim, none spends all its time in water. Lizards live either on the ground or in trees. Some lizards make their homes in underground burrows.

*Lizards bask in the sun to increase
their body temperature*

WHAT THEY EAT

Lizards are generally **insectivorous**. That means they mainly eat insects like flies, ants, beetles, and grubs. Most lizards also feed on plants if there are no insects close by. Some of the lizards that live in the African deserts eat only plants. Some lizards eat shellfish, meat, and birds' eggs. Certain monitor lizards are large enough to kill and eat pigs and deer.

Huge monitor lizards called komodo dragons eat pigs and deer

Some lizards have brightly colored throat fans

Green lizards have beautiful bright emerald skins

FRILLED LIZARDS

Brightly colored frilled lizards *(Chlamydosaurus king)* live in Australia. They get their name from a large piece of skin that hangs around their necks like a frill. When frilled lizards are angry they make the frill stand up like an umbrella. This is meant to frighten **predators** or enemies. Frilled lizards are some of the few lizards that can run on just two of their four legs.

Frilled lizards are found in Australia

FLYING LIZARDS

Flying lizards *(Draco)* are another strange lizard species. They are sometimes called flying dragons. Flying lizards live in the jungles of the Far East. They can fly up to twenty yards from tree to tree, usually to escape predators. Flying lizards' wings are made of skin supported by five or six long ribs. The wings are folded against the body until the lizard spreads them to fly.

Flying lizards fly through the trees

THEIR DEFENSES

Lizards defend themselves from predators in several ways. Some are covered with thick scales and sharp spines. Others depend on bluffing their way out of trouble by showing brightly colored parts of their body to their enemies. They may show the inside of their mouths, or flash a bright orange or blue **dewlap**, a flap of skin, as a warning. Many species let their tails fall off, which takes attention away from themselves. The tails soon grow back.

This lizard has lost its tail

BABY LIZARDS

Most baby lizards hatch from eggs laid in the ground. The eggs are kept warm by the sun until they hatch. If the eggs get too cold, the babies inside will die. A number of lizards bear live young, the eggs hatching as they are laid. This normally happens in colder places where the sun is not hot enough to keep the eggs warm. The eggs are kept warm inside the mother lizard until they are ready to hatch.

A baby green lizard hatches from its egg

THEIR SENSES

Most lizards have good eyesight. Lizards use the brilliantly colored parts of their bodies to attract or frighten each other. This means that they probably see in color and not in shades of black and white. Many lizards have a keen sense of smell. Their tongues feed scents to special sensors called Jacobson's organs. These organs are located in the roof of the mouth. The Jacobson's organs analyze the scents and send information to the brain. The lizard now knows what is nearby.

GLOSSARY

analyze (AN a lyze) — to find out what something is by studying it carefully

dewlap (DOO lap) — a flap of skin at a reptile's throat that is often brightly colored

insectivorous (in sek TIV uh rus) — insect-eating

molting (MOL ting) — shedding skin

predators (PRE duh turz) — animals that hunt other animals for food

reptiles (REP tiles) — cold-blooded, often scaly-skinned animals

species (SPEE seez) — a scientific term meaning a kind or type of animal

INDEX